HERE COME THE MOONBATHERS

ALSO BY PATRICIA YOUNG

POETRY

Traveling the Floodwaters
Melancholy Ain't no Baby
All I Ever Needed Was a Beautiful Room
The Mad and Beautiful Mothers
Those Were the Mermaid Days
More Watery Still
What I Remember from my Time on Earth
Ruin and Beauty

FICTION

Airstream

HERE COME THE MOONBATHERS

HERE COME THE MOONBATHERS

PATRICIA YOUNG

POEMS

BIBLIOASIS

FIRST EDITION

Library and Archives Canada Cataloguing in Publication

Young, Patricia, 1954-
    Here come the moonbathers / Patricia Young.

Poems.
ISBN 13: 978-1-897231-43-2
ISBN 10: 1-897231-43-1

    I. Title.

PS8597.O67H47 2008   C811'.54   C2008-900201-6

Edited by Daniel Wells

Illustration by Heather R. Simcoe: *Out of Their Element*

Canada Council   Conseil des Arts
for the Arts   du Canada

ONTARIO ARTS COUNCIL
CONSEIL DES ARTS DE L'ONTARIO

We gratefully acknowledge the support of the Canada Council for
the Arts and the Ontario Arts Council for our publishing program.

PRINTED AND BOUND IN CANADA

CONTENTS

For Connie

GRIEVOUS ROAD

All our dark thoughts carry us back
to that hearth on Grievous Road, the night
our mother washed dishes while our father dried.
He stacks plates on the table and when
the work's done
bends close to her face,
                              drops
a towel over their heads.
Beneath this damp tent
they laugh and kiss. Un-
                              conceived, specks
of dull matter, we curl
inside the cutlery drawer, listen
to our grandmother storm in and out,
swinging her cane.
Someday we'll get dirty
playing in her ashes
but right now we're innocent
as butter knives,
                    so small
we fit the curve of a spoon.
We don't care she slams doors,
locks herself into the pantry
to thrash about with her polio limp
and splendid insomnia.
                              It's too late
to worry whether we'll be born.
Already we're hungry for the sounds of earth:
the rasp of our father's match
as he lights a cigarette,
                              our mother's frantic
roll call
to make sure no one is missing.

THE DAY THE PIGS GOT LOOSE

A man in high boots strides over the grass.
Slap of a cricket bat, wood against pig haunch.
A dog runs the edge of the field,
the crow riding its back like a small black queen.

Slap of a cricket bat, wood against pig haunch.
And everyone's cheering like it's afternoon football.
The crow riding the dog's back is a small black queen.
My cousin turns to me and we kiss like movie stars.

And everyone's cheering like it's afternoon football.
Kiss against which all kisses will be judged and found wanting.
The youngest turns to me and we kiss like movie stars.
Where hast tha been since I saw thee on Ilkley Moor ba't'at.

Kiss against which all kisses will be judged and found wanting.
It's been years since I heard my father singing
Where hast tha been since I saw thee on Ilkley Moor ba't'at.
He's coming up the rear, herding the pigs toward the sty.

It's been years since I heard a man sing
to a dog, running the edge of a field.
They're coming up the rear, herding pigs toward a sty.
My father in high boots striding over the grass.

BUSTED

For singing in the school stairwell,
you and the Chinese grocer's
anorexic daughter. In the principal's
office she removed her black
hair as though a stiff hat.
It was Biology
you'd escaped,
the frog's heart and surgeon's tools.
How do we learn to forget?
she sang long ago
in the school stairwell,
her bald head and unblinking eyes.
How indeed, the principal answered,
before sending you back
to your formaldehyde classroom.
Though for all you knew
the grocer's daughter
might have been asking,
What does death taste like?
She might have been
singing to the trays
of tailless amphibians,
their brains washed
in dying light.

CAMP-OUT

We don't know where we're going, just that we're following
our father through the light and shadow of the northern
wilderness. At a crosswalk he holds out an arm. In front of us,
a bear and her cubs forage through a mountain of garbage. We
keep walking. Sandra, the kind one, carries a sack of potatoes.
Bess keeps stopping to pull burrs from her socks. Somewhere,
our mother, wrists strapped down in a hospital bed, screams for
her hands. In how many picture books have we seen trees
hollowed out like this one, windows and stairs and lanterns of
welcome? A sign hangs from a branch: *Where the crow flies her
tail follows.* We sit on the steps. Wait and wait while inside the
inn our father drinks beer. The stars blink on and he wafts out
the door with an Eskimo doll dressed in snow pants and a little
blue parka. Real fox fur rims the hood. On a riverbank we set
up camp for the night. At six years old I adore the canvas smell
of a tent as much as I adore anything. Bess rocks her doll by
the fire, pinches its hard plastic cheeks. In the cold light of
morning I wake to the sound of splashing water. Somewhere
our mother has given birth to a shrivelled infant we'll call Baby
for years. *How old are you? What's your favourite colour? Can
I blow out your birthday candles?* Questions I ask Sandra, who
refuses to answer. I kick the back of her legs. She inflates,
becomes a hot air balloon. Our father begs her to come down,
in long johns he begs and pleads and promises to one day
take her to a hockey game. Hotdogs, buttered corn, the sweat
of men.

BEFORE SLEEP, A CONVERSATION

Death is hard work, he says, *and the greedy greedy heart can't get enough.*
Of living, he means, of being alive.
She says, *I was thirty-eight before I got it –*
I mean, really got it – that I'd die too.
That sucking sound isn't the river, he says, *it's the sound of us dying.*
Quince reminds me of death, she says. *Sweet. Sort of woody.*
Who'd have thought dying would require such stamina, he says.
The inverse of childbirth, she says, *the concentration, the puh puh puh.*
Promise not to die in spring, he says.
If I go first.
The lucky few go to sleep one night and never wake up.
That was my grandfather.
But don't worry, he says, *death can't separate us.*
I'm not worried, she says, remembering the vow he made as boy,
to hunt her down in the afterlife.

AFTERHOURS

The waitress falls asleep on the floor and the chef's wife whispers,
Panic not, mothers of the brave new world.
A man who's spent his life tearing up his life motions with blue hands.

He's an out-of-work actor trying to keep it real.
And the sous-chef's in love with the chef.
The waitress sleeps on the floor and the chef's wife whispers,

This guy, this guy's the man.
The chef offers free martinis to anyone still standing
and the one who's spent his life tearing up his life motions with blue hands.

The chef adores the royal family. No one can explain this, least of all his wife.
Three in the morning and snow melts on her eyelids.
The waitress is sleeping so the chef's wife whispers,

Bring on the dancing elephants.
The sous-chef carves her name on a tombstone beneath a red sky
and the blue man tears up his life while motioning with his hands.

Darling, the chef says to the sous-chef, then turns to his wife:
When is it okay to call a woman darling?
The waitress, asleep on the floor, the chef's wife whispering:
This man's spent his life tearing up his life; now he motions with blue hands.

THE BONE CLOCK

– for H.R.

You had a lot of guts back then,
the bone clock said, that night in August.

*

We lie down.
We get up.
We lie down.
Bone clock, how long
can this supine sickness go on?

*

The fact of the bone clock
says more about death
than sex, she thought,
wanting a child
with the next good-looking
telephotographer.

*

If only the bone clock would cease its vigilant silence.

*

Why the bone clock?
Who the bone clock?
What to say about the bone clock
except it stopped when the world was still caterwauling
tooth and claw.

*

Between chipped gold columns
the bone clock's face
looks down from on high.
Always ten past four.

*

Another gin and tonic, she trilled,
from inside the mosquito netting.
Only the bone clock heard her cry.

*

If this poem is about anything
more than a mouse-infested cabin
in which a few animal bones
are scattered around
a broken clock,
                                pray tell –
what is it?

*

No tick.
No tock.
Not the slightest
interest in minute or hour:
no wonder we're cuckoo
about the bone clock.

*

Think: water
flowing through a clock
the way time
harrumphs
through our bones.

*

Hey, that wasn't the bone clock
chiming twelve times,
that was a squirrel
sharpening its teeth
on the deer
antler above
the front door.

*

In the heart of the bone clock three dead wasps.

*

Bored with old age, they lie on their backs,
staring at the kaleidoscopic water stains on the ceiling.
The bone clock remembers an ivory mantle.
Mother, it says. *Father*.

BOYFRIEND, LONG DEAD

You hear about girls gang-raped
at parties, a lacrosse or maybe

a rugby team, punk misogynists
who assume the world's their big fat

oyster. Girl on her third Southern Comfort,
a cliché, troop of adolescents

traipsing behind her up the stairs
to someone's little sister's canopy bed,

and how could you not hear
Camille Paglia in the background,

her staccato rapid voice:
You stupid stupid girl. And what about

those two, listening to *Dark Side of the Moon*
on the turntable beside his bed,

passing a bottle of wine back and forth
as though wine were just another

beverage, and then somehow they're
skin against skin and she's saying,

Let's do it, what's the deal, anyhow?
But then he isn't there, is somewhere

else in the room, pulling on jeans, *No,
not like this,* guiding her

back into clothes, tying her shoes,
both of them stepping outside,

cold slap of air, weaving down the street,
and every time I think

about that boy, I want to thank him
for being who he was,

an ordinary kid, no feminist or saint,
thank him for refusing

.   that girl, just asking
for it, begging to be shucked.

FALL

I fell asleep and when I woke, whoa, I was falling
out of a tree with long swooping branches.

My arms and legs jerked. I crashed
through a blur of nattering crows.

My nostrils blew smoke.
Where my ears should have been

there were thermostat knobs.
Fried salamanders, I was plummeting

at an incalculable speed. I went flat out.
Look ma, I shouted, *the suicidal dive!*

I crouched into a ball, dropped like a proverbial stone.
How quickly the brain adapts, the brain

adapts quickly. Metaphorically speaking,
I opened my wings. Or was my synthetic plumage

the metaphor? And then I was idling
like a Bluebird cab. There was time to ponder,

reminisce, the people I'd known – Gildners,
whole family crushed on the Hope-Princeton highway

en route to a wedding. Through a telescope, I spied
five Scottish dancers standing at attention.

The wind lifted their kilts as though lifting
tail feathers. The air smelled electric.

In the outdoor bandshell a piper droned.
The world fell quiet. My tongue tasted of clay,

the bottom of a clay-bottomed lake.
In my diary I wrote: *August 7th, tumbling head over heels.*

Fish raining alongside, mostly sardines.
That's when my childhood rushed up to meet me:

those feverish nights, swimming back and forth
through the eye of a needle. For a while

I forgot my descent at incalculable speed,
then forgot I'd forgotten.

I turned to the landscape, the jagged coastline
and nameless white flowers.

Became engrossed in a door-stopping novel.
Fist in the air, tears in my eyes, I longed for

a hobby, knitting or golf, anything
to distract from a future of post-collision vehicles,

space junk falling from the sky.
I recognized my mother's handwriting,

scratched on the hubcaps, life's truths,
the very things she'd been trying to teach me!

In my diary: *All peaceful now the flag's hauled down.*
The Scottish dancers leapt (I held my breath, I waited)

and when they didn't come down, people yawned,
shook the grass from their blankets, yes,

there was my mother, young, jet black hair,
walking out of the park, along a street

where an ice-cream truck
had rung its bell only moments before.

At the front gate she groped in her pocket
for a key that wasn't there. *If it's not one thing,*

it's another, she said, and hiked up
her skirt to climb the cedar tree

at the north side of the house,
tree with long swooping branches.

She climbed for days, weeks, the months
passed like marriage vows. And when she was parallel

to the glassed-in porch on the second floor
she pulled herself onto the ledge.

I'm in, she called, voice
disappearing through the missing pane.

DESOLATE THE GOOSEBERRY

The rain won't stop falling. It falls.
Hour after hour while our father floats in a drugged coma.
He's waiting for my sister to fly back from Hawaii.
Which teaches us something

about having a life: sometimes you can decide
when to kiss it goodbye. It's been months since the sun
turned the world yellow. Now a man drowns
in his own lungs. On the deck,

wrought-iron chairs hold out their watery sleeves.
Desolate the gooseberry bush, desolate the willow tree.
Summer's elsewhere, a butterfly behind glass.
Cars speed past the house, throwing

small oceans in their wake. Once, my sisters and I
were the grasshoppers of August, our father
at the record player while we leapt
across the lawn. At the end, our mother drags

a bed into the living room, the doctor brings oxygen,
morphine floods our father's brain.
The mailman tramps to the corner,
sack bulging beneath the waterfall of his cape.

TWENTY QUESTIONS

At seventy-six Mum discovers she's pregnant.
No, I say, *impossible. How could it happen?*
She shakes her head, she doesn't know, doesn't care,
says, *Don't just stand there, go get your father.*

Grey myself, I remind her he's been dead eighteen years.

Go, she says again.

He's wandering the cemetery, a sack of bones
I haul up the back steps. On a chair by the oil stove,
he belches acres of dirt, takes his time arranging
and rearranging his mostly decomposed limbs.

Well? he says. *What's she selling this time?*

I want to give him the facts, tell him straight up
but she says, *No rush, let's play a guessing game.*

Bigger than a breadbox? he says. *Smaller than a proverb?*

No, she says. *Aye.*

Speak with a forked tongue?
Heal like a wound?
Batten down its hatches?

Dad smells of mulched leaves, something sweetly organic.
Pulverized beach shells spill from his eye sockets.

Sing like a goat? Shatter like a plinth?

Mum winks at me, spreads her hands over her stomach.

Out with it, he says, *I haven't got all day.*

Twins! she says, and his head snaps up
like a moon on a stem. In moments they're young again,
but he's eyeing the door.

Hold your horses, woman.

Is it like jury duty?
What are my options?
And if I say no?

SCREECH OWL

What I saw down at the dock:
thin brown shoulders, the back of her head.
She was thirteen. In a silver boat
her brother rowed into the lake.
All month the screen door slammed.
At night the walls of our room breathed,
hot and alive. Or was there something
under the bed, something with heart
and lungs, some sound
we could not identify
in all our years of living?
Down at the dock she looked up
from her book: three times a day
her brother fished for trout,
his back bent like an old man's.
In the fire pit we grilled corn, potatoes,
vegetable kabobs. The inexplicable
hiss, in and out, dark exhalations.
I searched closets, drawers,
finally pulled back the curtain.
A goggle-like face heaved close
to my own. *Whoosh*, it was gone.
After that, whenever I turned my head,
wings lifted off water, our daughter
looked up from her book. Down
at the dock, her shoulders, for instance:
thin and brown.

ALPACA FACTS

From the top of Beacon Hill my husband and I
look down on the unbroken meadow stretching to the sea.
He's wearing the alpaca coat my father bought in England
before immigrating to Canada, true north cold and free.
We came up here to look at the geographic marker:

38 lines pointing in 38 directions.
In 1954 my father paid £42 for the coat,
the price of a half-decent second-hand car.
Of this my mother never failed to remind him.
Walking around the circle, I keep the Olympic Peninsula

in sight, Mt. Rainier, 75 miles distant, Mt. Baker shimmering
in my sweet spot. Everything else I keep up my sleeve.
Rain drumming on a tin roof sounds nothing
like an alpaca kicking its softly padded feet in high thin air.
Since the marker's installation in 1950 a few notable buildings

have been torn down. *Time*, my husband says, *ain't she
a wrecking ball.* What was my father, son of an East Yorkshire
farmer, doing in an import clothing shop in London?
Even the hyper-allergic can wear alpaca wool,
which comes in 22 natural colours. After his death

in 1987 my mother gave the coat to my husband.
At 6' 2" he's the same height my father was. Some articles
of clothing are so beautifully tailored they transcend
the whims of fashion. Alpaca farmers love their animals
and claim their animals love them back. Descended

from the wild vicuna, they make a humming sound when happy,
like a swarm of bees. My father arrived on the west coast
of the continent in a heat wave, $300.00 of borrowed money
in his pocket. The centre arrow, pointing to True North,
is as accurate today as it was the day he stepped off

a train in Vancouver, wearing this ankle-length, satin-lined coat
made of a luxurious grey fibre. On my husband it is a rather
regal-looking garment. Tribes in the Andes once practiced rituals
around the alpacas' death: a person of honour would plunge
his hands into the animal's chest cavity and rip out

its heart. For a while it felt like my father had just gone away.
The night I knew he wasn't coming back, I sat up in bed
and howled. I was 33. Alpaca facts: strong, warm, light, soft.
Knowing nothing of the Mediterranean climate,
my parents pinpointed the southern tip of this island,

then made it home. This morning my father's passport
photograph appeared on my desk. Who put it there?
Why? His eyes seem to say, This is my location:
48 degrees North Latitude, 123 degrees West Longitude.
He told my mother he felt like a *right dafty* wearing the coat.

So he didn't. Talk of cross-breeding gets you thinking, doesn't it?
Alpaca and bee? Striped wool, silken hum, 22 shades
of honeycomb? Memory is full of microscopic air pockets
whereas my father's eyes in the photo are piercingly exact.
The arrow pointing to the North Magnetic Pole

hasn't been accurate since the middle of the last century.
Once, in a dream, I walked into the strange and bloody waters
of sacrifice and realized I'd been there before. In 1950,
City Hall paid $557.00 for this bronze circle installed
on a chest-high concrete cylinder. Some breeds cluck.

Others warble like songbirds. According to the farmers,
the love is in the fleece. *Forty-two pounds was a small
fortune back then*, my mother said, draping the coat
over my husband's shoulders that winter morning.
For that you could buy a half-decent, second-hand car.

JACK(S)KNIFE

I am lost to you in the corner of a board and batten house far from anywhere.
The grass grows tall as a child and the sunlit trees rise like tapered candles.
Your hand, my blade: together we carved out the hour
between blackberry picking and the moon's eclipse.

The grass grows tall as a child and the sunlit trees rise like tapered candles.
Before you left, you searched for me in every drawer and pocket
between blackberry picking and the moon's eclipse.
But now the star-clustered sky gapes between us.

Before you left, you searched for me in every drawer and pocket.
Behind the coal box my mouth is jammed with steel
and the star-clustered sky gapes between us.
How I loved the rub of your thumb along my wooden haft.

Behind the coal box my mouth is jammed with steel.
In dreams I make my way back to you on a day when the sleet falls sideways.
How I loved the rub of your thumb along my wooden haft,
the way you'd dance with your wife to big band records.

In dreams I make my way back to you on a day when the sleet falls sideways.
Who will discover me among the dust balls and bits of plastic alphabet?
How you'd dance with your wife to big band records!
Such is the happiness seen only in movies.

Who will discover me among the dust balls and bits of plastic alphabet?
Your hand, my blade: together we carved out the hours.
Such is the unhappiness seen rarely in movies:
to be lost to you in a board and batten house far from anywhere.

LIVE TRAP

Mice are haunted by beauty but have no time for it.
Too busy gorging and shitting and eluding
capture or death. Smart little buggers,
and cute too, though non-discriminating.
There's nothing they won't sink their pointy

teeth into, including shoe polish and soap.
Your average mouse spends its high-octane
life shuffling off this mortal coil. Once,
you held one in your hand, its hummingbird
heart. *There, there,* you whispered,

take it easy, little guy. Not what you say to
your seven-year-old son in his *poom do bok* gi.
Goddamn kid moves through molasses.
Mice sail down the Nile in halved
walnut shells. Or dash up the wainscotting

before dissolving into peepholes from which
they peep back. Far-seeing and fatalistic
but also capable of Houdini-like feats. Watch
that one flatten like an envelope, melt into
the tableau. Mice confess to moral failings

and shameful rage. *Get your slow ass
in gear,* you say to your son, nudging him
out the door. Christ! Late for school
and soccer and now tae kwon do. Mice
are chameleons: one minute a woodland sylph,

the next a rat. If, while you sleep, mouse
ribbons slither across your face, say nothing
to the neighbours. Like dentists or psychopaths,
mice lack a crucial piece of the personality
puzzle. Heaven is just one place they feast

on sweet buttered corn. *Time must be*
different for me, your son cries, slumping
to the car. *It always feels like I'm going fast.* Shape-
shifters, turd-droppers, mice are the first to admit
the asexual life forms do not start wars. Listen

to them toss around grandiose strategies,
the sole purpose of which is to finagle the scraps
from your plate. Every kid on the block
wants to be a ninja. To razzle-dazzle with high-
flying kicks. Mice are fleeting, not here

for a long time. Despite their savoir faire,
they tumble like the class clown into your trap.
Blink and the bucket's empty. Bamboozled
again. Mice light up the mind's nether regions,
always an afterimage, the thing that just was.

OLD MAN'S BEARD

On a vinyl barstool I dipped and swerved
above the city, looking down on cathedrals and control

towers and tiny people, and there was
my daughter swathed in that green gauzy stuff

that clings to tree branches. Crazy kid,
she'd been in my purse, smeared lipstick over her mouth.

And she'd lost an earring, a cheap dangly thing
with a champagne-coloured stone.

With what would she adorn herself now?
Wait. That goat-faced imitation was not my daughter,

silly fruit bone, two feet tall and last seen wearing.
At the police station I provided dental records,

photographs, fingerprints, but police are the same
wherever you go – haunted and unwilling

to discuss crucial information. Back
on the barstool I soared above copper domes

and flying buttresses, scanning the city for one lost girl,
light as a cat and so bewitching . . .

YARD SALE

Last week Jilly flung another nest onto the compost,
cursing damn robin, its wing-bright industry,
not here, not under the deck, too much coming and going,
the barbecue, human traffic. The point is:
Lay your eggs elsewhere.

Blue all winter, she's sunny at last, washing beer
bottles at the sink, her son and six buddies manning the yard:
busted settee, Peter Pan lamp, unloved Ninjas.
Revved-up boys raring for cash, but so far
no-one's out of pocket. She's out of her funk,
knocking the window: *Hey, that's my good
axe, you can't sell my good axe.*

It's all got to go, don't look at the sky
to read the future, and still no sign of a buyer, oh, here
comes old Tom, collector of curios and curiouser.
Wicked deals for you, sir, the freckled kid's saying,
identical twin popping a wheelie around
Tom's hobbling girth. Every dollar counts
but how to sell a dead man's shoes to another with one foot
in the grave, honey mustard leather, size eleven?

The clouds go bankrupt, the twins roll on the grass
with the big black dog: *Get off our chest!* Tom
flipping through books, *Our Bodies/Ourselves,*
poor blushing man sold down the river.

Rain's spitting hard now, too late to stem
the drift into wreckage and ruin,
someone singing somewhere:
Don't get me to the church on time.
And Jilly under the deck, sorting through junk,
pausing to look up, and there in the rafter,

perched in a nest the size of a soap dish –
cheap bird ornament, made in China? If not for
the quivering tail feather, defiant black eye.

NOCTURNAL

Here come the moonbathers in their shiny bikinis with the ruffled bums.
Here they come on skinny legs, knees dipping as they walk
toward the bulrushes. See them slide off the rocks into
gelatinous black water.

*

Wasps thrum above the lily pads, hunting aphids.
All day, the neighbour's boys,
                    thundering human cannonballs,
hurl themselves off their dock.

Cattails stand phallic in the sun.

*

Last summer the moonbathers turned on noon's buttery spit.
Ten minutes on one side. Ten on the other.
In the ultraviolet glare they sipped fizzy lemonade,
read trashy magazines.
                    (*Burn baby burn*)
But now they're hip to the dermatologic damage,
wise to the moles threatening
to hatch tiny brown
spiders
on the downy
smalls of their backs.

*

Asleep all day but here they come now,
                    ruffled, skinny, in shiny bikinis. See them
enter the moonlit spaces
                    along with
        the okapi
lynx
        vampire bat.

THE WOMAN WITH AN EPIC-SIZED HEART

Looked a lot like me right down to the plump earlobes and scrawny wrists. You're thinking twins but it was nothing like that. We talked and drank saké in tiny blue cups. Mars Water Bombers flew so low they grazed the tips of the fir trees. The woman was insubstantial in the bodily sense, though she must have had some kind of body. Those were knees, after all. My heart is small, you see. Sick with hurt and petty complaints. Her lack of substantiality might lead you to think she was a ghost or apparition but that would have meant she'd died and death cannot live inside an epic-sized heart. It's hard to explain what exactly she was or if the smoke wafting through the forest was beautiful or terrifying. The planes, on the other hand, were just what they seemed – heavy and bloated as Thanksgiving turkeys. I looked the woman in the eye and told her things I'd told no one, a lifetime's worth of lurid confessions and then the canvas umbrella burst into flame. Some kind of synchronicity? Despite our similarities, her skin was new. She'd had a facial, she said, the top layers exfoliated. I leaned close, and, yes, she did appear sort of waxy and stunned.

CANNIBAL

We did not talk about death as he lay there
dying. Though once, near the end,
he turned his strangely beautiful
face toward me, and asked:
What does it mean
to dream a severed head? As though I
could interpret the unconscious
thoughts of one so ravaged
by life, so close
to death. By then, he could not
stomach food. For weeks, had subsisted
on air. He said he was dancing
with the severed head, filled with an uprushing
happiness. His eyes were large,
the way a baby's eyes
are large: an otherworldly visage.
I saw him, then,
waltzing around a courtyard,
dappled sunlight, bird wings splashing.
He said, *And then I realized my dancing partner,*
the severed head,
was my head, but even this
did not disturb me. His joy irrepressible
as he dipped and turned, arm
outstretched, hand cupping the head,
which had shrunk
to a small wizened thing, a dried
apple, perhaps – soft, fragrant. I leaned
forward, took his fingers in my own.
What happened then? I asked.
He smiled, the tip of his tongue
vibrating against the ridge of his front teeth:
I was hungry, of course,
so I brought my head to my mouth
and I ate.

MEXICAN WEDDING

The guests sang, hundreds of them,
walking out of the church behind a twenty-eight year old
virgin dressed in white lace. No one knew
the words but words didn't matter.
At sea level my voice is damp and monotonous
but in that high clear air it took on an exultant tremolo.
In the great hall with no windows:
five men in pink suits,
a miriachi band playing *La Cucaracha.*
Fog rose from the dance floor.
Someone's idea of heaven? I asked
the old caballero. *Dry ice,*
he laughed, and I wished I'd been born
in that village, in the pine-crested mountains,
among those people. Girls wearing pineapple crowns
delivered platters of tortillas, tamales, fish
caught that day from Lake Patzcuaro.
Children everywhere. At midnight
we pinned honeymoon cash
to the bride's veil and groom's lapels,
while the waiter with the cruel
and beautiful face of an Aztec king
plunked a bottle of tequila down on each table.
Hot sauce, hip action, sun-beaten cowboys
doing the salsa. Four in the morning:
walking the cobbled streets,
bone tired, a little palsied dog leading the way.

MELT

"We can't even describe what we're seeing."
                    Chair of the Inuit Circumpolar conference.

One morning they appear in nameless droves.
Fabulous creatures flicking their silver fins and ancient jewels.

A long lost mythology? Weird migration?
They lurch onto the tundra like bawling infants,

announce themselves with the subtlety of a brass band.
Wave upon wave, antlers vibrating, tails ablaze.

Who? we ask. *Who are you?*
One day they aren't there and the next

they're traveling toward us
with the speed of a birchwood forest.

We gather to mourn those passing
swiftly into memory, the polar bear and arctic seal.

Time cracks.
The century is thinner than ice.

We have 1200 words for reindeer but not one
for hornet, robin, elk, salmon, barn owl.

Try to understand: we have never seen a barn.
Never stepped into such a cavernous space.

*

We'd never stepped into a cavernous space.
Try to understand: we'd never seen a barn.

Hornet, robin, elk, salmon, barn owl.
We had 1200 words for reindeer but not one

for a century thinner than ice.
Time cracked.

Swiftly into memory: the polar bear and arctic seal.
We gathered to mourn those passing

with the speed of a birchwood forest.
They traveled toward us –

one day they weren't there and the next
we asked, *Who*? *Who are you?*

Wave upon wave, antlers vibrating, tails ablaze.
They announced themselves with the subtlety of a brass band,

lurched onto the tundra like bawling infants.
A long lost mythology? Weird migration?

Fabulous creatures flicking their silver fins and ancient jewels
appeared one morning in nameless droves.

ADOPTION, 1962

Let the nuns say there's no one to blame
but yourself. Let them say it's all
for the best, he'll be happy with this couple

and their underground sprinkler system,
an army of gardeners bending and snipping.
Let these men tend to the camellia bushes,

each rusted blossom and blade of grass.
Look around, nothing to clutter up
the eye, even the telephone wires run

underground. Let this man and woman
take you by the hand, past the dizzying
walls of art, up the marble staircase

to a light-filled room where they'll show you
neatly folded infant jackets, a row
of sterilized bottles. The wallpaper is

sailboats, the crib empty. If only you could
focus, see beyond the yellow
ducklings, fuzzy white clouds.

*

Panicked, the nun scans the room.
A pregnant woman waddles toward the piano.
The nun says, *There's a girl, give him to me.*
The woman sings, *The old grey mare, she ain't what she used to be.*
Rain hits the glass. The nun presses forward.
A struggle? Some kind of tug of war?
Kicked at the whiffle tree, kicked at the whiffle tree.
You pass him to her, as though to say,
Where did I get this? Here, you take it.

*

In the apartment above
college boys play bridge and drink whiskey
in the last scraps of dawn.

Your breasts ache milk
but no pearl
nestles

in the curve of your body.
No small squirming thing latches on.
Now and then the boys

lay down their cards, shout obscenities
from the balcony,
though when you pass them

on the street,
they're always polite,
they never swear.

*

It's summer and light splinters the sidewalk.
The little mothers in running shoes and ponytails
push strollers up and down the avenues.

Already they've become terrible busybodies.
Today on the bus you heard a mewling
cry and your nipples stung. Tears?

You looked around. *Tears?*

*

Your life's barely begun. There's so much ahead!
The kind nun whispered this before you left

Our Sisters of Mercy in your puffy jacket with
the faux fur collar. It's what you whisper to yourself,

standing at the extreme reach of the breakwater,
blunt point of reference that feels more like an end.

*

In time you'll marry a patient man
with a photographic memory.
You'll give birth to four girls –
Maureen, Laureen, Kathleen, Sharleen –
and just when you think you've finally moved on
from your minor adolescent
indiscretion, you will reach for him,
the one you nursed
in the many-chambered dark. Just
when you think you cannot remember
the colour of the hospital walls you'll remember
green glycerine
soap, the bite of fresh linen,
engorged breasts, a peevish-looking Christ
looking on.

*

You invented all of it –
the couple with the broad pleasant faces.
The swing set and dog.
Even the house with the mansard roof.
Its shiny red door.

SEPTEMBER TRAIN

Crossing the canyon, you look out the window,
see the train's shadow creep over the trestle,

a bug inching along a branch. Blur of rock
faces, green foliage sliding into warehouses,

cement blocks, and now you're travelling
behind small box houses, beneath canopies

of maple and arbutus. That's when you see him:
boy on a picnic table, waving both hands.

Children do this, they do it all the time,
wave at the trains flashing past their backyards,

three, four times a day, bodies flung out
in the guttering light – *It's me. Here I am.*

This one's whole life a backdrop behind him –
mother, father, baby sister wailing because.

You don't see what he's wearing or the look
on his face. You wave back but already

he's gone. It's like everything, it happens
too quickly, coming down the island, whistle

blowing and you thinking slow thoughts.
That boy. He's there. And then. He isn't.

MIRACLE OF LANGUAGE

A deer steps into the long green evening. Quivering ears and velvet eyes
stare back at my face, white as a plate at the bedroom window.
Tonight, a forest diorama: trees, moss and rock.
Once my daughter woke from a nap in this same wallpapered room

and stared at my face, white plate in the bedroom window.
Flushed, rumpled, attuned to bird-music,
she woke from a nap in this same wallpapered room.
Twenty-eight years ago she called me from the summer kitchen,

flushed, rumpled, attuned to bird-music.
When I came through she was sitting up in the Queen Anne bed.
Twenty-eight years since she called me from the summer kitchen,
then uttered her first string of words,

sitting up in a Queen Anne bed. When I came through,
her arms opened like a perfectly formed sentence.
I don't remember her first string of words,
but in the moments that followed, I thought, Who are you,

arms opening like a perfectly formed sentence?
Tonight the forest's a diorama of trees, moss and rock.
Stopped in the moment, I wonder, Who are you,
stepping into the long green evening: quivering ears and velvet eyes.

FIRST TRIMESTER

Driving through town, half listening to the radio, you glance at
Cosmo Girl on the passenger's seat – *Luscious sex for a luscious
body!* – thinking drug store pregnancy kit, how reliable, and do
you have the right change? You turn up the volume. It's an
astronomer describing a new high resolution stereoscopic
camera. Even as a child he was entranced by Mars, red planet,
seventh largest, fourth from the sun, and you, what did you feel
when Miss Parkinson pulled down the map of the solar system?
Awe? Boredom? Hunger for the saltine crackers you'd unwrap
at recess? Waiting for the light to change, you imagine the
astronomer a small boy with dark curls, boy baffled by other
boys, their baseball cards and pop guns, imagine him removing
the centrefold from National Geographic, pinning it above his
bed – nine multi-coloured globes set in black space, each hard
and pure as a marble. And now he's remembering his twelfth
birthday, the book from his grandfather – *Mars: Fact and
Fiction*. How desperately he wanted to believe the *canali* –
those thin dark lines the Italians saw through their telescopes
meant little green men lived underground. Which is where you
are now, in a parking lot beneath a medical clinic, the
astronomer saying, *All I want to know, all I've ever wanted to
know – was Mars warm and wet like earth? Billions of years ago
was it hospitable to life?*

BOOMERANG

Beside my mother's grave I lay down and slept.
Spring. Freshly turned dirt.
That was then. This is now.
On a cemetery bench three drunks howl at what?
Suddenly everyone's an existentialist.
A feeding frenzy churns up the bay:
squid, herring, octopus.
Will the sleepwalkers please go back to bed?
December 31st. Help! Life is fatal.
Climb onto this raft of bones.

*

Outside Lucky Bar, Monica's hair goes meteorological.
A cop ambles over, breathes down Mick's neck:
Hey Bub, any beer in that pack?
Instructions on how to throw your boomerang:
turn at a 45 degree angle.
One New Year's Eve we attended a fancy dress ball
at the old Crystal Gardens.
Ten years ago? Twenty? Last century
city workers planted a garden of imported trees.
Spanish fir. Cork bark elm. Chinese plum.

*

Soggy soggy bottomland.
No wonder cremation's the new big thing.
Not to mention the art of the urn.
If at birth we'd been given a map of our lives
would we have followed it? Bits of broken clay
around a potter's workshop rendered the land useless.
I have excised three lines involving dark grey clouds.
How beautifully they bleed into a less grey sky.
Well, that's that then, another year
saunters off, whistling.

*

The cop pulls six cans of beer out of Mick's pack.
Well lookie here. Monica's
corkscrew curls go *boing boing boing.*
Before the seawall was built storm waves washed out low-lying graves.
My granddaddy's buried right here,
one of the drunks shouts as we walk by.
If the wind is blowing off the water, face the water.
If the wind is blowing off the desert, face the desert.
Tomorrow we'll take stock,
make vows we can't keep.

*

Me in pearls and itchy taffeta.
You in pleated trousers, gold watch on a chain.
The past has ceased to be. The present exists.
The future's yet to happen.
Pretty obvious stuff. Nevertheless. Sea lions
bark in a seaweed stew, their smooth heads.
If thrown horizontally,
your boomerang will zoom up sharply,
then dive to the ground. Together, Mick and the cop
pour perfectly good beer onto the grass.

*

Ghoulish fact: kids circa 1911 played
with buckets, shovels, clavicles, shin bones.
This morning no one cares to unstitch the quilt of life.
Mick forgets where he is, what he's doing.
Fireworks explode in the inner harbour.
He pauses, takes a sip. Waste not, want not.
Aiyee, baby no, Monica cries, too late.
Impart spinning motion as boomerang leaves your hand.
Already yesterday and the day before
bob like amphibious shapes in fog.

*

Alcohol equals happiness.
Acetaldehyde equals hangover.
Trapped in the here and now, we exist beyond it.
Bittersweet conundrum.
Should'na done that, the cop says to Mick
who politely asks if he might undrink it.
'Fraid not. To obtain more spring,
hold between index finger and thumb.
Monica dislikes the idiotic word
games people play at parties.

*

In some part of his pickled brain,
Mick understands all events exist
on a scale of earlier and later.
What's history? What's myth? What's the difference?
Us, hopeless, feet tripping over big band music.
If thrown correctly your boomerang will follow
an elliptical course, return from the left side.
This milestone is just another day, or is it?
A TV cop would've pulled a gun.
Nobody moves. Nobody gets hurt.

*

After big storms, corpses buried along the sea bank
would rise up. O wrath of grapes.
Mick lies on the kitchen floor, a baby bird, mouth open.
Monica feeds him strips of toast with honey.
Now is no more or less real than a minute ago,
or a thousand years to come. Admit it:
thinking's absurd. No panacea for a hangover
apart from suicide. *Ham-let,* Monica says,
that was the answer. Open the curtains.
The light on the water has changed again.

*

If you were destitute, stillborn, a convict, woman
of ill-repute, descended from a race
other than, your coffin might float away.
Ancient paradoxes lead to mathematical notions
but don't solve the problem of a $200.00 fine.
My mother was the only person I know
who could use the word *pagan* and mean something by it.
Try to imagine no sense of a present
that will become a future generations' past.
Be still like a Buddhist. Practice mindfulness.

*

Okay, okay. What's Kant's take on time and space?
Which comes first: reality or experience?
Is the bottle made to fit the shape of the wine?
Are the moments goldfish leaping from our hands?
Monica: *Are we playing another guessing game?*
From a great distance, Mick observed himself
taking an expensive sip of beer.
Clue: Shakespeare's little piglet.
The polar bear swim has been cancelled
due to lack of polar conditions.

*

For heathens and them without
the sense God gave them: Potter's Field.
With this tea strainer, drink at the font of life.
To obtain accurate results, aim at something
in particular but always live
forward, understand backward.
Stars press against the glass ceiling.
On a summer afternoon the cemetery's the calm eye
at the centre of the world. As your boomerang
comes to you, clap between your hands.

*

Long ago we fled palm trees, carp pools,
a talking parrot with a black pellet tongue.
Gone before the kisses, champagne pop.
The first day of the year comes and goes.
If left-handed, use a left-handed boomerang.
See above instructions. Imagine the world in reverse.
Three tempests in three weeks equals
wreck and ruin. If Mick doesn't pay
within fourteen days, interest accrues.
Stare into the fire. Send in the angels.

*

Time and space are not elements of reality
the mind tries to comprehend
but features of the mind we use to
comprehend reality. So said Kant. Apparently.
Hamlet on the other hand addressed poor Yorick.
Alas. Those kids down at Ross Bay
tossed sun-bleached skulls into the air.
This morning the ground's so wet tree roots can't hold.
If your boomerang fails to return to you,
do not lose hope.

*

What is it about good old boys singing in a graveyard?
Should auld acquaintance be forgot?
The chance of coming into existence is infinitesimal.
Briefly, briefly, the mind burns incandescent.
I woke on a tombstone, not far from my mother.
Chilled to the bone. Lips burnt.
Aren't we all half in love with easeful death?
Her last words: *Don't call. Don't write.*
Oh to be on a fast-moving train,
going somewhere new.

MISTRAL

Life as it happens is too much for us, he said, so we asked what he meant by too much and he said the mistral and the hot dry wind funnelling down the Rhone Valley through a gap in the Pyrenees. Walking a dusty road, we'd fallen into step. He said a woman's name; it sounded like Janine. He described a Babel of tongues, madness, a donkey's ear torn off. The Napoleonic law, he told us, had once excused crimes of passion when the Mistral had been blowing for more than three days. *Who's Janine?* we asked, and he repeated her name in such a way that we guessed he was in love. It was too much. This old man in love! Crossing the train trestle, he told a story – ten stone houses perched on a hillside. Inside one of them, a woman in tears. *Her husband, who'd just left her, was gay, you see, though gay was not a word people used back then.* We smiled at his embarrassment, then felt ashamed. *When I tried to console her, she laughed and said, Non, non, Je pleure de bonheur pour lui.* He paused to catch his breath. He put one foot unsteadily in front of the other. *Brain-scattering,* he said. *Gibbering. Idiot wind.*

ICEMAN

I want your pure alpine seed and prehistoric
DNA. Want your chalcolithic baby. Fuck me
in some hollow crag. No one will ever know
we climbed so high, beyond ecstasy and material
decay. Who were you –

shepherd in winter, guiding your animals down a mountain pass?
Outcast in grass cloak and goatskin leggings?
Were you tracking game above the treeline?
Caught in a sudden storm?
Before death

you spread your things around you
just as I spread mine each night before bed –
water glass, sleeping pills, eye drops, bracelets.

For five thousand years you lay belly down
until a Saharan wind storm
blew tons of fine particles as far as the Alps.
Over summer, dark grit absorbed the sun's rays,
melting the glaciers. A German couple
saw your head sticking out and thought
a doll! How could they know

there is poetry in a well-preserved corpse,
in the isotopic composition of a tooth's enamel?
Even your eyeballs are intact.

This is where I turn away, here
at this mountain crest, where hikers took turns
jabbing you with sticks and ski poles.
Your terrible saviours, jack-hammering
a hole through your hip. When finally
they hauled you free, it seemed
your genitals were missing.

Sit up. Smile for the cameras.
You are front-page news.
King Tut's a child compared to you.

One woman claims to séance you nightly.
Another, unhinged, writes to the newspaper,
querying the viability of your sperm.
Can it be thawed? How beautiful

your 57 tattoos located on 57 acupuncture points.
Tiny x's like tight sinew stitches.

Scientists have done all they can for you:
measured, X-rayed, carbon-dated, microscopically
analyzed tissue and gut contents.
In the South Tyrol Museum you lie in cold storage
with your flint knife and unfinished longbow.
I stop to read the plaques –

chieftain ritually killed to propitiate the gods?
Stolen Egyptian mummy planted as a hoax in foreign ice?

Lately, your keepers talk of a violent skirmish.
What's clear – eons ago
something went very wrong
in the Otzal Mountains, something dark
and murderous, but look, none of that matters now
because I'm here, saying, Come to me
with your belly full of ibex, come with copper
and arsenic streaking your hair, with your whipworm
infestation and the names of things
rattling like dried berries in your pockets,
an arrowhead lodged in your shoulder, a little tear
in your coat. Trader, shaman, warrior,

take out your flint and pyrite, charcoal and tinder fungus.
I am that half-mad woman, saying,
Let us make fire.

DIVORCE FEVER

We fell out of love, all of us,
at the same time, last day of winter,
crocuses poking through dirt, yellow and mauve,
trees turning an excruciating green.
A spell cast over the happily married heartland,
even the old ones, the shrunken couples
who couldn't walk or swallow
or see the fingers snapping in their faces,
even they were blowing apart.
One morning we woke, divorce in the air,
a song everyone was singing.
A sweeter deal, a fresh kick at the can.
For a while, we spun through the cycles,
took out the garbage, hearts knock-
knocking through the kids' recitations.
Outside the lawyer's office, we told jokes
and drank daiquiris. Slip us through
the loopholes, make it iron clad
and legal. Every time we turned around,
a scrappy little river dog
had clamped another
dead-duck marriage
between its jaws. Spring,
then summer, then hopped up
on tango lessons, we didn't notice
all the commotion had interrupted
mah-jongg and mealtime,
carpools and swimming classes.
The gardens went to hell.
And no one paid attention or the water
bill, no one scraped the bird shit
from the windows. No one
heard the kids choke on stolen
bubblegum underneath the stairs.

MOTHER TONGUE

Tonight my aunt recites my uncle's terrible
transformation. Three years since his stroke
in Wales and then the long journey back
to speechlessness. *Baa,* the sheep bleated

in the fields. *Baa baa black sheep.* He's a big man,
the right side of his body dead as the sister
whose funeral he'd flown half way
around the globe to attend. I want to

show my aunt the birds' nests I've built with spit
and mud and tears, but she's reading a book
up on the bluff. Now and then she lifts her eyes
to see my uncle trudging through the forest,

a small coffin on his back. She can't drive
so buses across the city to visit him seven days
a week in extended care. He loved that
there was always more work in the garden –

beets and gladioli, rhubarb galore. The words
she's reading are stunted creatures that sigh,
So and *Ah ha.* My aunt remembers the smell
of dry leaves in his hair the afternoon he slid

out from under the cabin where he'd been
checking the log foundation for rot. I am
trying to say something about dignity
in the face of loss – my uncle lifting an index

finger for *yes.* Nothing for *no.* And the names
he can't utter. His own. Hers. She turns
to a story about a boy who falls in love with
bonsai, while revisiting the sequence of events

that day in the farmhouse: my uncle pushing away
his tea cup, climbing the stairs after a breakfast
of fried eggs and kidney pie, hand gripping
the banister, three more steps to the bathroom,

where he looks in the mirror and considers
soaping his face, but suddenly shaving's too much
effort even for his favourite sister's funeral.
I wake and it's summer. In each nest

a small miracle rubs against a great sorrow.
The air's a soft lullaby, which is what my mute
uncle sings in his wheelchair, eyes closed,
Suo Gan, word perfect in his mother tongue,

lyrics moving effortlessly through an open
pathway of his brain: *Ni cha dim amharu'th gyntun/
Ni wna undyn â thi gam.* Harm will not meet you
in sleep/Hurt will always pass you by.

DELUGE

And it came to pass, when men began to multiply on the face of the
earth, and daughters were born unto them, that the sons of God
saw the daughters of men that they were fair, and they took them
wives of all which they chose. – Genesis 6: 1-2

I walked a long way in an old pair of sandals
and when I looked up
I saw the fiery shape of a man
revolving in a field of blue space.

My knees locked, my tongue split like a flame.

In those days the world was immaculate
and devoid of memory.
It was difficult to think
without hearing
the language of birds.

His face emerged slowly,
feature by nascent feature.
And then his neck/chest/thighs –
all perfect, all splendidly formed.

He put on a body of flesh
as though putting on a suit of fine cloth.

Roses bloomed over the dip
of thorny hills and my eye cocked
toward Paradise.

                    *

Where had he come from?

I didn't know, nor did I ask
if he'd been sent to me as some kind of
balm for the curse of being human.

Standing in the dark, braiding the horse's mane,
I'd feel him lean into the blank
pools of my thoughts. He was
clean intelligence, incandescent.

Sex with an angel?
my sister said, pulling
water from the well, her voice
dipped in arsenic.

I no longer knew what I was –
woman or jackal, fish or flying thing.

       *

A restlessness seized him.
He grew pale, spoke of the place he'd forsaken,
his words the same swollen sounds
scratched on the walls outside Eden.
And then the gibberish in his sleep –
the sky bursting open like a goat-skin bottle,
the ark's wooden doors
slamming shut.

       *

Those final days –
walking among the aloe trees,
leaves trembling like my senses.
The nightingale drunk on his beauty.
The giraffe weeping as he passed.
Bees clung to his skin. Everything
from the protozoan to our hybrid son
banging his breakfast bowl on the table
appeared resplendent and tragic.
I understood even the lowest embryo
manifests will, desire, a terrible cunning.

       *

Death by drowning.

Should he have warned me, I whom he could not save?
Should he have whispered that last night of love –
When the rains finally come I will pass through your world
like the voice of an animal.

TORMENTA

What is the purpose of your visit?
Do you plan to stay three days, three weeks or three years?
Your boyfriend, waiting in Arrivals, has told us
you intend to slip over the U.S. border
under the cover of night. If you deny this
he will deny you. Why the grimace, the curling
lower lip? Would you like us to send for a translator?
Yes is the wrong answer. So is no.
Were you wearing those high-heel boots
when you boarded the plane in Mexico City?
Your apparent disinterest in our questions
only heightens our suspicions. We don't mean
to imply that you are a bad person,
but would you stand over there by the wall
while we go through your luggage again.
If we dump out this coffee what will we find?
Is Michoacan a province or state
and can you find it, blindfolded, on a map?
How many times have you smuggled
cocaine into this country? Don't lie to us. It insults
our intelligence. We apologize
for the stale air, lack of windows.
What aren't you telling us?
The only translator available
is eating dinner on the north side of the city.
Our advice: answer every third question
in the affirmative. Whatever you say
your boyfriend has already contradicted you.
We have been tracking your internet correspondence
for years. Every email is in our files.
Consider this a heads up.
No, you cannot sneeze.
No, you cannot use the washroom.
Why do you insist on feeding us a line?

Ignore the flickering lights and concentrate, please.
Your Euro-American features tell an interesting story
of conquest and defiance. It's so easy
to contradict oneself, isn't it? The storm
raging outside has been upgraded to a hurricane
and the translator's car battery has gone dead.
List all the jobs you've been fired from because of
pregnancy or theft. Why the eye-rolling, the sneer?
Do I need to remind you that we are highly trained
professionals who can read the illicit desires
of even the most taciturn criminal. Why
are you more beautiful than the woman
in your passport photograph? Who
is the impostor? It seems a tree has fallen
on the translator's car, crushing the front end.
How much longer can you keep up this silence?
We've just received word that your boyfriend has left the airport.
A major bridge has collapsed, a forest has been flattened,
No, you cannot have a glass of water.
No, you cannot sit down. There goes the power
but don't worry, we can continue
this interview in the dark.
We know you know something about something
so why not confess?

EXTINCTION

Three hours between flights but we have coffee, magazines,
earplugs to muffle the airport, as always, under construction.
We stare at photographs of Antarctica, lose track of time.
Now and then look up. Passengers arrive in ones and twos.
Out comes a laptop, diaper bag, cell phone. A chunk of ice
the size of France breaks off without warning. The seas rise
dramatically. The banging's louder now, more insistent.
Hammers, drills, some kind of rattling. Turning, we see a man
spread-eagled against a glass wall. Like Dustin Hoffman at the
church window. In love and out of his mind. How long his
pounding, mouth a silent howl, ignored by hundreds, maybe
thousands, rushing from terminal to terminal? Through glass
he tells us he took a wrong turn after disembarking. A door
locked behind him. *A fucking labyrinth back here,* he informs
the pretty custodian we bring over to help. Lacking authority
or tools to set him free, she radios someone who radios
someone else, a security guard in a golf cart. *Get me out of here,
I'm gonna miss my flight.* The custodian makes soothing
motions with her hands while the security guard punches
numbers into a keypad. Departure time approaches. The
lounge fills with freshly-coiffed members of the world's
doomed flying club. A crowd gathers, all eyes on the flailing
specimen in a three-piece suit. He loosens his tie, sobs great
gulping sobs. Official-looking people appear though no one
can access the code that will let the man out, let us in. A voice
announces: passengers at gate 33 will not be boarding Flight
AC 1742 after all. We have never witnessed such unabashed
despair. Never looked at anyone the way we look at the man
behind glass.

SKELETAL

How long till they break down the door,
find my bones surrounded by unopened
Christmas presents? The electric
heat clicks on and off. A tap drips,
junk mail swims through the slot.
To pass time I sing little ditties:
Ding dong. I'm so far gone. I'm a maggot's song.
I make bets with myself: five days, eight
months, ten years. This morning
anything seems possible, even
discovery. Sun and moon muddy the windows
and then it rains so hard the leaves
beyond the glass turn crisply green.
When they enter, will they cover their faces,
shy dogs circling an animal's remains?
Will they verify my smile with the smiling photo
on the mantel (yes, those are my teeth)?
Rummage through my drawers, fingering
underwear and pill bottles? How,
they will ask, could this woman's absence
go unnoticed three years? How
could she become so unglued from her life,
and what was the life from which
she'd become unglued? On the street below
buses stop at red, lurch forward at green.
A jackhammer tears up the pavement.
Natural causes? Foul play? I imagine
the pathologist, a stout French Canadian
with a fondness for old blues records
and *Fin du Monde* beer, stepping
onto the balcony for a lungful of air.
Death, he will say. *She is no great mystery.*

LETTER FROM THE DEAD: A RESPONSE

Friends, nothing has changed/ in essence.
        Affonso Roman DeSant'Anna, *Letter to the Dead*

And here, things also go as they go.
No kitchen cabinets or boys
suffocating in submarines at the bottom of the sea.

No flat tires.

We enter each other with an absorption only the elephants
(yes, they are here too) understand.

The bartenders still tell the best stories.

No need for sledgehammers or private detectives.
We carry no spare cash. As always,
we try to avoid despair and pushy salesmen.
Jousting matches, hunger, twenty-five-year mortgages–
nothing more than intriguing ideas.

Travel is no longer a destination;
we exist in all the quaint villages at once.

No evidence of a Stone Age, a War on Drugs.

Just remembering the family dinners –
passing crushed turnips around the table –
sends us running along the flagstone river path.

Oh, it's not as dull as you imagine.
We bowl for points and the cocktails have names like *Blue Ether*.

We manage fine without digestive tracts, pornography.

At the juncture, where the beanstalk grows beyond the red rooftop,
the extinct creatures, the leopards and dolphins,
turn up to remind us. Remind us of what,
you might ask, you might ask if the animals here can talk
and if so, what do they say.

We like our indifference toward winning or losing,
our extreme position on fossil fuels.

Imagine a summer afternoon where no one's called *Babyface*.

From where we're sitting (high on the bleachers)
it's hard to take seriously our former shenanigans.
Evenings we wile away the time, making bets
on what you'll do next: another flophouse, another prison?

We smile (though never cruelly) at your naive belief–
that you lie at the centre of all the great mysteries.

Our language is breathless; I mean it requires
no breath. We are tolerant of obscenity and trust you
will learn all the lyrics. Have I mentioned
the sun rarely sets and everything
we do
we do for the first time?

Come quickly.
We have prepared a room for you, laid out clean bathrobes.

Odd I should say this
when *bathrobe* (along with *adolescent, pyramid, flunky*)
has dropped from our tongues.

As for the streetcar,
I haven't seen it pass this way in years.

IN PRAISE OF POETRY (OR WHY I STOPPED WRITING IT)

With thanks to Bernard Welt

I stopped writing poetry when Irene
told me that Jarkko told her
that he and his family used to drive

out to the country every Sunday afternoon
to sit on a long wooden bench
facing relatives sitting on a long

wooden bench. No one spoke.
Clock ticking. Dog asleep on the
braided rug. Sat like Quakers except

they were Finns, and then Jarkko's
family would get up, put on their coats,
return to the car, drive back to the city

(in silence) where they'd eat dinner
(more silence), then go to bed
(protracted silence). What could a poem

possibly say that hadn't already been
said on an ordinary afternoon inside
that farmhouse outside Helsinki?

*

At last I'd grown up.
I could walk, talk, eat with a fork.
I had nothing left to say.
I asked myself:
What did you think
you were doing
pouring your fool heart
into stanza after stanza,
lo those many years?

*

Do you need another tortured simile?
Do I?
Does your great Aunt Hilda in her saggy baggy hose?

*

Re poetry: I ceased and desisted when my daughter (age eight)
announced she was turning to prose. She'd had it with the lyric, its
bittersweet longing. No more gimmicky flimflam cockamamie
tomfoolery for her. No sir. She was going to tell it straight. She sat at
her little desk and pounded on the keys of an Underwood typewriter,
circa 1964:

*Overwhelmed with joy, Emily listened as her parents talked with the real
estate agent. They had been trying to make her into a lady for some time
now. Her family was rich from a canned vegetable product: PAPPY'S
STEWED TOMATOES.*

I wanted the real estate agent to trick Emily's parents into buying a
mansion riddled with termites (that would teach them for going on
about what a swell guy he was). I wanted Emily to grow up fast. As
the heiress of a canned tomato fortune she was sure to fall into a life
of treachery. I wanted this treachery to become inexplicable and
darkly sexual. I wanted Pappy, stubborn old bastard, to use the word
"conflate" in a complex sentence, using the subjunctive verb. I
wanted him to go to his grave without revealing the secret ingredient
(sugar) for his success. I wanted the market on canned tomatoes to go
bust just as Emily discovers her long lost twin sister is making a
killing on crushed pineapple. No, scrap that. Corn nibblets.

*

I stopped writing poetry because an unrhymed couplet made as
        much
sense as prayer and I didn't have the faith to walk through that door.

*

My mother's death shocked me speechless.
At her graveside I infant-babbled. The piper played
Amazing Grace beneath a blue spruce.

It began to spit rain.
Out of nowhere an undertaker appeared.
It was a poetic moment

and if death weren't the body blow it is
I'd have scratched a haiku on a piece of bark
to commemorate the occasion:

> *Sudden spring rain. Pink*
> *umbrellas opening. Wet*
> *skin stretched over bone.*

*

The last Bengali tiger ground up for penis soup
was more than a poem could bear.
I spat out
every human sickness that end-rhymed
with aphrodisiac –
hypochondriac, megalomaniac, insomniac,
kleptomaniac, nymphomaniac.
I could go on . . .

*

I quit cold turkey but I was hardly the first or most original.

*

Let the kids crank out the doomsday anthems,
assault the senses, sing the black lotus, wreak the havoc,
scribble the portentous image, reverse the dumb logic, repeat
osseous, osseous, osseous is the bleached driftwood
in relation to the hot white stones.

*

A geisha is NOT
     (never has been
          never will be)
              as guileless as the moon.

*

I was tired of trying to rationalize
my moral failings in language
designed to confound the reader
in such a way that the concept
of sin inevitably manifests itself
as a means of water transport.
Think: small wooden dory.

*

After slogging through forty-nine
books of verse which began with I –

I am a prairie snowstorm.
  I am a grain of sand.
    I am a no-nonsense ass-kicking love machine –

a clamp fell over my mouth.
I flailed like a Jack stuck in its box.
I stammered: *I I I.*

*

Dusk crept
up my skin.
Hours passed.
Then morning.
Then noon.
Another sun
beat down.
I don't know
how or when
but life without
poetry
became almost
acceptable
to me.

*

No poetry but I still needed love.
Hey, honey, I said, *there's been a dearth of good loving*
around these parts for some time now, hell,
why don't we order us up a big juicy platter.

*

No matter how you crunch it
a damned and dull-eyed devilled darling
is a damned and dull-eyed devilled darling is
a damned and, etcetera.

*

What do you do when you wake up to discover
your perfect life is not a poem after all?
Hop on a motorbike, proceed without headlights?
Smuggle yourself out of the abandoned city?

Your perfect life is not a poem after all.
Which is fine except your blood is full of magnets.
You'd like to smuggle yourself out of the abandoned city
but you're stuck to the fridge. You're a radiator dying of rust.

Which is fine except your blood is full of magnets.
Hop on a motorbike and proceed without headlights
while stuck to a fridge? The radiator dying of rust
wakes up and discovers you. What do you do?

*

It hit me.
Poetry was like hopscotch.
One day I was nuts about it.
The next
I couldn't see the point.

*

Bend your ear to the earth. Listen.
The carpenters of the world are walking through the last forests,
subtracting words:

Pine is the white bread of wood.
Pine is the white bread.
Pine is the white.
Pine is.
Pine.

*

last confession:
i stopped writing poetry
when i heard the mighty thrum of insects
which some say is god

i quit my lower-cased scribbling
i became distracted
i am distracted still

ACKNOWLEDGEMENTS

Thanks to the Canada Council, British Columbia Cultural Services, and the University of New Brunswick's Writer-in-Residency Program for their support.

"In Praise of Poetry (or why I stopped writing it)" owes a debt to Bernard Welt's "I stopped writing poetry," published in *The Best American Poetry 2001*.

"Boomerang" was inspired by "Stop all the clocks," an article in the *Independent*, (London), by Julian Baggini.

Thanks to the following magazines in which some of these poems previously appeared: *Arc, The Fiddlehead, Grain, The Malahat Review, Prarie Fire, Prism International* and *Room Of One's Own*.

"Busted" was published in *Long Journey: Contemporary Northwest Poets*, edited by David Biespiel.

"Deluge" and "Campout" were published in *Breaking the Surface*, Sono Nis Press.

"Melt" was published on the Parliamentary Poet Laureate website.

"Campout" and "Twenty Questions" won *Grain*'s prose poem competition on separate occasions.

"Live Trap" and "Screech Owl" were selected as finalists in *Arc*'s Poem of the Year contest on separate occasions. "Screech Owl" was chosen as an Editor's choice.

"Miracle of Language" placed second in *Room of One's Own* poetry contest.

"Fall" and "Letter from the Dead: A Response" were nominated for National Magazine Awards by the editors of *The Malahat Review*.

I would like to thank the following people for their editorial suggestions over the years: Michael Kenyon, Carol Mathews, Jay Ruzesky.

Thanks to Heather Simcoe for her woodcut on the cover of the book, and to Dennis Priebe for his care and patience in typesetting and design.

Special thanks to Dan Wells, wise and generous editor and publisher, and to Terence Young for his love and friendship and everything else.

ABOUT THE AUTHOR

PHOTO: TERENCE YOUNG

Patricia Young is the author of eight books of poetry, and one book of short fiction, *Airstream* (Biblioasis, 2006). A two-time Governor General's Award nominee, she has also won the Pat Lowther Memorial Award, the Dorothy Livesay Poetry Prize, the CBC Literary Competition, the British Columbia Book Prize for Poetry and the League of Canadian Poets National Poetry Competition. She lives in Victoria, British Columbia.